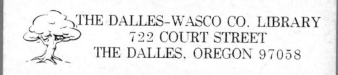

The Wolf
Will Not Come

The Wolf Will Not Come

Myriam Ouyessad • Ronan Badel

Schiffer Kids™

4880 Lower Valley Road, Atglen, PA 19310

Other Schiffer Books on Related Subjects:

Mabel and the Queen of Dreams, Henry, Joshua & Harrison Herz, ISBN 978-0-7643-5137-2

Originally published as *Le Loup Ne Viendra Pas* by L'Elan vert, Saint-Pierre-des-Corps, France © 2017

Library of Congress Control Number: 2019935973

Type set in KB Reindeer Games/Full Sans/Andika

ISBN: 978-0-7643-5780-0 (hard cover)
ISBN: 978-0-7643-5876-0 (soft cover)
Printed in China

Published by Schiffer Kids
An imprint of Schiffer Publishing, Ltd.
4880 Lower Valley Road
Atglen, PA 19310
Phone: (610) 593-1777; Fax: (610) 593-2002
E-mail: Info@schifferbooks.com
Web: www.schifferbooks.com

For our complete selection of fine books on this and related subjects, please visit our website at www.schifferbooks.com. You may also write for a free catalog.

Schiffer Publishing's titles are available at special discounts for bulk purchases for sales promotions or premiums. Special editions, including personalized covers, corporate imprints, and excerpts, can be created in large quantities for special needs. For more information, contact the publisher.

We are always looking for people to write books on new and related subjects. If you have an idea for a book, please contact us at proposals@schifferbooks.com.

"They did not know it was impossible, so they did it."
Mark Twain

To Ronan B., who fulfills dreams with the stroke of a pencil.
M. O.

For Arsène.
R. B.

"Go to sleep, my rabbit."

"Are you sure the wolf will not come?"

"Very sure."

"How can you be so sure?"

"There are no more wolves. The hunters have chased them away."

"And there are none left?"

"Yes, there are still some, but not many."

"Then, how can you be sure that one of those wolves will not come?"

"The remaining wolves are hiding in the mountains, far away from here."

"I thought the wolves were hiding in the woods."

"Yes, the wolves are hiding in the woods that are in the mountains."

"Mom, there is a woods not far from here. How can you be sure a wolf is not hiding in those woods?"

"That woods is very small, you know. A wolf could not hide in it."
"But if it's a wolf who knows how to hide? A wolf who knows how to stay out of sight?"
"Even if a wolf was hiding in that woods, he could not come here."
"How can you be sure?"

"To come here, he would have to come out of the woods and cross the city. Thousands of people would see him!"
"Mom, what does a wolf look like in real life?"
"It looks like a big dog."

"Then maybe people would mistake him for a big dog."
"Maybe, but even if people thought he was a big dog, the wolf could not get here."
"How can you be sure?"

"There are too many cars in town. The wolf would be hit by a car."

"You know, Mom, a wolf who escaped the hunters, who came from so far away, who managed to hide in the tiny woods . . . he can probably sneak between the cars."

"Probably, but even if the wolf did not get hit, he would not make it this far."

"How can you be sure?"

"This city is huge! It's a real maze, with thousands of streets that look alike. The wolf would not find our building."

"And if the wolf had our address?"

"Wolves cannot read!"

"But they are clever! Maybe he could figure out how to find our building."

"Maybe, but even if the wolf found our building, he could not get in."

"How can you be sure?"

"There is an entrance code, and the wolf does not know the code to open the door."

"And if the wolf was waiting for someone to come in . . . Father Pinaud, for example. He has the code. Also, he doesn't notice anything! The wolf could enter behind Father Pinaud without being seen."

"It's true that Father Pinaud is completely unaware of what's going on around him. But even if the wolf snuck in behind him, he would not get to our apartment."

"How can you be sure?"

"We live on the fifth floor, and wolves do not know how to take the elevator!"

"Mom! Do you really think that a wolf who has already managed to do all this will stop because of an elevator?"

"Listen, Rabbit, even if the wolf came up in the elevator, he would not get in here."

"How can you be sure?"

"I am sure! The wolf will not come. And now, you have to sleep. Goodnight, my rabbit."

"Goodnight, Mom."

Knock, Knock, Knock

"It's surely the wolf!"

"Happy Birthday!"

"I was sure you would come!"

About the Author

Myriam Ouyessad was born in 1976 in Paris. After studying philosophy at the Sorbonne, she chose to teach the youngest. She participated in the creation of the alternative youth magazine *From the Water to My Mill* in 2011, where she also published her first stories.

About the Illustrator

Ronan Badel was born in 1972 in Auray, Brittany. A graduate of Decorative Arts of Strasbourg, he began writing and illustrating children's books, publishing his first book in 1998. After several years teaching illustration at a Paris art school, he settled in Brittany and devoted himself to creating children's books. In 2006 he published his first comic book, *Petit Sapiens*.